This Makes Me Sad

DEALING WITH FEELINGS

by Courtney Carbone
illustrated by Hilli Kushnir

Random House  New York

I made a big mistake.
I left the gate open.
My dog, Kit, ran away.

Now I have
an awful feeling
inside of me.

I tell Mom and Dad what happened.
They tell me it will be okay.

But I do not feel like it will be okay.
I feel like I lost my best friend.

We get into the car.
We drive all around town.
But we cannot find Kit.

The sun sinks in the sky.
My heart sinks, too.

Mom and Dad make
a lot of phone calls.
No one has seen Kit.

It is almost dinner time.
But I am not hungry.
I feel like there is a rock
in my tummy.

It is a rainy night.
The raindrops look
like tears on my window.

I start to cry.
Dad tells me it is good
to let out my feelings.
I do feel a little
better afterward.

11

It is time for bed.
Mom and Dad tuck me in
with a teddy bear.

It is soft and warm,
just like Kit.
But it is not the same.
I miss my best friend.

The next day,
we put up signs
all over town.
I see lots of people
with their dogs.

My insides feel
like ice cream melting
in the hot sun.

Later, we drive
to the animal shelter.

Kit is not there.
Mom gives them a sign.

I look at the animals.
I have an idea!

We can collect supplies
for the cats and dogs!

Mom and Dad love
my idea!
They tell everyone
we know.

20

Soon our house is full of food and supplies for the cats and dogs!

We bring everything
to the animal shelter.
The staff is thrilled!

The dogs bark.
The cats meow.
Hooray!

Mom asks them about Kit.
No one has seen her yet.
I feel funny inside.
I stop to think.

It feels good
to help the other dogs.
But I feel bad
that Kit is still lost.

I have so many happy memories of Kit.
But they no longer make me feel happy.
I feel like a piece of me is missing.

What am I feeling?
I am feeling SAD.

I close my eyes.
I see Kit in my head.
I can even
hear her barking.

I open my eyes.
I cannot believe it.
Kit is really here!

A woman found Kit playing in her yard!

She is safe and sound.
It is time to bring Kit home!
Hooray!

For kids everywhere, that they may find
wonder and joy in being themselves
—C.B.C.

To Liam and Aya, whose occasional
teary eyes make me ever so SAD
—H.K.

Text copyright © 2018 by Courtney Carbone
Cover art and interior illustrations copyright © 2018 by Hilli Kushnir

All rights reserved. Published in the United States by Random House Children's Books, a division of Penguin Random House LLC, New York. Originally published by Rodale Kids, an imprint of Random House Children's Books, a division of Penguin Random House LLC, New York, in 2018.

Step into Reading, Random House, and the Random House colophon are registered trademarks of Penguin Random House LLC.

Visit us on the Web!
StepIntoReading.com
rhcbooks.com

Educators and librarians, for a variety of teaching tools, visit us at
RHTeachersLibrarians.com

Library of Congress Cataloging-in-Publication Data is available upon request.
ISBN 978-0-593-43423-9 (trade) — ISBN 978-0-593-43424-6 (lib. bdg.) —
ISBN 978-0-593-43425-3 (ebook)

Printed in the United States of America
10 9 8 7 6 5 4 3 2 1

This book has been officially leveled by using the F&P Text Level Gradient™ Leveling System.

Random House Children's Books supports the First Amendment and celebrates the right to read.

Penguin Random House LLC supports copyright. Copyright fuels creativity, encourages diverse voices, promotes free speech, and creates a vibrant culture. Thank you for buying an authorized edition of this book and for complying with copyright laws by not reproducing, scanning, or distributing any part in any form without permission. You are supporting writers and allowing Penguin Random House to publish books for every reader.